Chester's Presents

Written by
Mitzy McNease

Illustrated by
Kim Cox

Blancmange Publishing
Sweet Books

Printed in Hong Kong

Chester loved Christmas
more than a little.
He made out a wish list
for skates and a fiddle.

But it didn't stop there.
It went on for miles.
This list was enormous.
It gathered in piles.

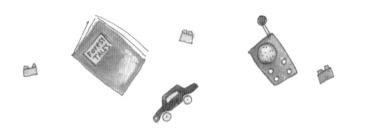

Chester was a master
at finding the things
he didn't have yet
for Santa to bring.

As Christmas came closer
he asked his mother,
"May I open just one—

and maybe ...

another?"

She quickly replied,
"No presents for you—
not yet little one.
It isn't quite Christmas.
Santa's not done."

With each passing day the list grew longer.
Even his begging grew stronger and stronger.

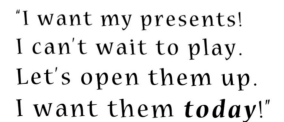

"I want my presents!
I can't wait to play.
Let's open them up.
I want them *today*!"

"You must wait for Christmas,"
she sighed. "I know it is hard.
Your presents will keep.
Go play in the yard."

Outside by the stump
of the great old willow,
Chester found his friend, Benny,
holding a pillow.

"I want to open my presents under our tree.
My mother said, 'No,'—she won't listen to me!
Have you asked to open a present you found,
under the tree, just lying around?"

"No," answered Benny, "there are no gifts under our tree.
I only get one—from Santa to me."

Chester was puzzled. "Only one present?
Just one single box?
Why not a pile of lots and lots?"

"I'm not quite sure," Benny replied, "but I don't really mind.
I can make my toys from the things that I find."

"What kind of present do you usually get?"
asked Chester, still not believing Benny just yet.

"Sometimes a coat," said Benny, "or shoes for school. Once it was my very own brush with a sparkly green jewel."

"Don't you want more
than those sorts of things,"
asked Chester, "like baseballs and yo-yos
and maybe a swing?"

"That would be grand," said Benny,
"to get a real toy this time.
A toy I don't have to share—
something just mine.
But Santa only has room
for the thing you need most.
His bag is already so stuffed
he can't get it closed."

Chester lie in bed thinking that night,
about his friend, Benny, and it didn't seem right.

He pulled out his list to look over the markings,
making quite sure there was enough for his stocking.

Quick as a flash he forgot about Benny
and added to the back... number one thousand and twenty.

As his eyes slowly closed he sang a song
he knew quite well from begging his mom.

"I want my presents, I ca

A few days later,
Chester sat quiet as a mouse,
watching Benny play
at his house.

His worn blue jacket
hung limp on his back.
His snow bootstraps
were fixed with a tack.

He laughed and played
with his siblings that day
with a flattened box
they used as a sleigh.

Chester gazed at his friend
wondering how it must be,
not to have presents
under the tree.

He suddenly remembered
the gifts he had
and thought of another
he wanted to add.

"I want my presents!
I can't wait to play.
Let's open them up.
I want them today!"

Christmas Eve came, sure enough.
And Chester knew he'd get lots of stuff.

He looked outside to the Rabbit's cozy burrow
and saw the whole family under the mistletoe.

No wads of wrapping paper covering the floor.
No torn string ribbon tangled galore.
No puffs of tissue to kick about.
No sturdy cardboard to fold and toss out.

They sipped their cocoa
in front of the fire.
Then sang Christmas carols
just like a choir.

On Christmas morning
Chester was up before dawn.
He quickly carried his presents
across the front lawn.

He tip-toed inside
the Rabbit's slumbering lair
and nestled his gifts
one by one there.

He and his mother sat by the window that day
watching the Rabbit family play, and play, and play.

It was the best Christmas ever, Chester had to admit,
"It's a good thing I knew just what to ask Santa for,
isn't it?"